Eight Days of Christmas.

Before embarking on her writing career, K.D.Ray completed a degree in teaching and has done many jobs from teaching in Primary Schools to driving a tractor.

Originally from Yorkshire she, now, lives in a rural village in Lancashire where she is currently working on her next novel. For more information about upcoming releases and to buy her debut novel
For The Best?
Visit www.kdray.co.uk

Eight Days of Christmas Copyright © 2018 by K.D.Ray. All Rights Reserved.

All rights reserved. No part of this book may be reproduced in any form or by any electronic or mechanical means including information storage and retrieval systems, without permission in writing from the author. The only exception is by a reviewer, who may quote short excerpts in a review.

Cover designed by Caitlyn Southgate

This book is a work of fiction. Names, characters, places, and incidents either are products of the author's imagination or are used fictitiously. Any resemblance to actual persons, living or dead, events, or locales is entirely coincidental.

K.D.Ray

Printed in the United Kingdom

First Printing: September 2018

Follow on Facebook – K.D.Ray

Website: kdray.co.uk
Designed by GadgetSmart.net

Acknowledgements.

Very special thanks to WITH YOU LOCKETS 54 Elizabeth Street Suite 2 Red Hook, NY 12571. Especially Troy for the help, inspiration, kindness and generosity.

I stumbled upon **withyoulockets.com** whilst researching the history of lockets for my opening story *Lisa's Locket.* It's a beautiful website featuring heirlooms for the future and the owners were so kind when I asked for their help with my story – even the cover of the book is down to them! Words cannot express my gratitude to these strangers across the "pond" who give true meaning to the saying "a stranger is just a friend you haven't met yet".

Special thanks to Maddy Lawrenson from Media by Maddy for my author photo.

Also very special thanks to Caitlyn Southgate for the photography and cover design of the book.

For my kindred spirit and the sister I never had –
Sharon.
Love you Mrs.O!

Lisa who believed I could do this even when I didn't.
I will always be grateful to you!

And everyone in my Inner Circle!
Especially Maing Maing and Brenda.
Xxx

Visit from St. Nicholas
By Clement Clarke Moore (1823)

'Twas the night before Christmas, when all through the house
Not a creature was stirring, not even a mouse;
The stockings were hung by the chimney with care,
In hopes that St. Nicholas soon would be there;

The children were nestled all snug in their beds;
While visions of sugar-plums danced in their heads;
And mamma in her 'kerchief, and I in my cap,
Had just settled our brains for a long winter's nap,

When out on the lawn there arose such a clatter,
I sprang from my bed to see what was the matter.
Away to the window I flew like a flash,
Tore open the shutters and threw up the sash.

The moon on the breast of the new-fallen snow,
Gave a lustre of midday to objects below,
When what to my wondering eyes did appear,
But a miniature sleigh and eight tiny reindeer,

With a little old driver so lively and quick,
I knew in a moment he must be St. Nick.
More rapid than eagles his coursers they came,
And he whistled, and shouted, and called them by name:

"Now, Dasher! now, Dancer! now Prancer and Vixen!
On, Comet! on, Cupid! on, Donner and Blitzen!
To the top of the porch! to the top of the wall!
Now dash away! dash away! dash away all!"

As leaves that before the wild hurricane fly,
When they meet with an obstacle, mount to the sky;
So up to the housetop the coursers they flew
With the sleigh full of toys, and St. Nicholas too

And then, in a twinkling, I heard on the roof
The prancing and pawing of each little hoof.
As I drew in my head, and was turning around,
Down the chimney St. Nicholas came with a bound.

He was dressed all in fur, from his head to his foot,
And his clothes were all tarnished with ashes and soot;
A bundle of toys he had flung on his back,
And he looked like a pedler just opening his pack.

His eyes—how they twinkled! his dimples, how merry!
His cheeks were like roses, his nose like a cherry!
His droll little mouth was drawn up like a bow,
And the beard on his chin was as white as the snow;

The stump of a pipe he held tight in his teeth,
And the smoke, it encircled his head like a wreath;
He had a broad face and a little round belly
That shook when he laughed, like a bowl full of jelly.

He was chubby and plump, a right jolly old elf,
And I laughed when I saw him, in spite of myself;
A wink of his eye and a twist of his head
Soon gave me to know I had nothing to dread;

He spoke not a word, but went straight to his work,
And filled all the stockings; then turned with a jerk,
And laying his finger aside of his nose,
And giving a nod, up the chimney he rose;

He sprang to his sleigh, to his team gave a whistle,
And away they all flew like the down of a thistle.
But I heard him exclaim, ere he drove out of sight—
"Happy Christmas to all, and to all a good night!"

∞ ∞ ∞

Introduction

Everyone has their own family traditions for Christmas and, as a child, I would be taken to one of the garden centres to look at the lights and Christmas displays. I was always allowed to choose one new tree decoration each year and, one year, I chose a tiny little book on a gold string to be hung on the tree. The book contained tiny illustrations and the words of the *Twas The Night Before Christmas* poem.

This became a tradition in itself. It would be the last thing to be hung on the tree and it would be read through before being given pride of place amongst the branches of our spindly green tinsel tree. I still have this book and I read it each year to my children before ceremoniously positioning it on our own more "realistic" artificial tree.

Some of my happiest and earliest childhood memories involve Christmas Day spent in the loving warmth of my grandparents' home. They had a small silver Christmas tree, lots of lights, a Christmas angel that I had dressed in tinfoil, a plastic sleigh and Christmas cards hung across a string pinned along "the big wall" in the lounge.

To this day, the smell of tinsel reminds me of Christmas day with them. We would arrive to find a small Christmas stocking under the tree which was filled with small gifts and lots of tangerines which my grandad painstakingly wrapped up along with the gifts.

Grandma would have a coffee break from preparing the Christmas dinner so that we could all open our presents together. I would usually be given practical presents like a new coat or a new dress and I dreaded getting new clothes because they always made me leave the warmth of the coal fire to go and try on my new things in the freezing cold hallway.

My favourite thing I got each year was a selection of little clothes for my Sindy and Barbie dolls which my Grandma knitted herself. She also used to make outfits and pram blankets for my Tiny Tears doll which I passed on to my own daughter when she was little.

Christmas dinner was always a busy affair and we had to use every chair and stool to fit everyone round the big table. We always had a little "table present" each waiting for us at each assigned place and a cracker which usually contained a little metal puzzle or a plastic clip-on moustache. Grandma brought the turkey through sliced up onto plates then let everyone help themselves to the bowls of potatoes and vegetables strewn around the table.

After the meal I would help Grandma do the washing up then we'd carry through all of the cakes she had made – she was an amazing baker and always made far more than any of us could manage. We always found room to manage a turkey sandwich later on though after we'd played cards, charades and "hide the thimble" which involved a lot of shouting of "warmer" or "colder" according to the proximity of the hidden thimble. Then I would usually end up falling asleep snuggled into my Grandma who also fell asleep from such a long day of making everything perfect.

I have since strived to make Christmas perfect for my own children with, admittedly, varying degrees of success. The way we celebrate Christmas and many of the traditions we uphold stem from Queen Victoria's reign. The tree, turkey, crackers and mulled wine are some of the Victorian features of a modern Christmas and, for some reason, I always feel under immense pressure to attempt to live out the dream of this Victorian Christmas idyll.

Each year I imagine slipping on a Bing Crosby Christmas CD to enjoy dressing the tree with my family then switching on the lights, in a ceremony akin to the Blackpool Illuminations switch-on, then sitting back in the warm glow to sip a sherry. To this date, this scene has never played out! The kids hate decorating the tree and usually end up in a ball of tinsel fighting over who gets what and who does what and I don't like sherry!

My point is – I really don't think that a Victorian style Christmas is achievable and I am certain that none of the Christmas films on the run up to the big day portray an accurate version of the celebrations of normal people. At least a month spent pushing and shoving round the shops fighting off bugs and germs and, when you have small children, the scuffle to get the latest must-have toy.

The food shopping, alone, takes weeks and no matter how rational you usually are it becomes imperative that you buy enough food to feed an army for the shops being shut over Christmas and the possibility that you may be snowed in. Add into the mix the annual visits to and visits from people you are unlikely to see for another year and the relatives that are forced to try not to fall out for one day.

It's all very, very stressful! For many years I have sat dejected and feeling like an utter failure for not achieving Hollywood's expectations of a Christmas family gathering – not having a family that looks like all the smiling, happy families on all of the TV adverts. In our family there's always someone who doesn't like what you've bought them and is rude enough to share their disappointment with you. Once, I was told "well the charity shop will be glad of it" after I had congratulated myself on finding the perfect gift that year for a very hard to please elderly relative!

So Boxing Day holds more allure for me. The hard work is all done and dusted. The house is all tidy thanks to the weeks of cleaning, clearing and decorating on the lead up. There are lots of recordings to catch up on and films to watch and no need to cook. The day is usually spent in pyjamas with duvets on the settee watching television or playing about with gifts we've received. We all just pick at leftovers from the day before and eat whatever we like. There are no rules or expectations for Boxing Day so it's always a success!

I have written a series of eight short stories with eight very different versions of Christmas. I hope you will enjoy them all and I hope that you remember that the images of Christmas which you see on television are not everyone's reality. Whatever your Christmas holds for you, I hope that you are spending it with the ones you hold dear and I wish you all a very Merry Christmas and a happy, healthy New Year.

Contents

Lisa's Locket.

Christmas Angel?

An Unforgettable Christmas.

Christmas Miracle.

Away With a Stranger!

Sally's Secret Santa.

What a Pantomime!

Christmas Beginnings.

Chapter One.

Lisa's Locket.

Lisa had always loved the idea of owning a locket ever since her mum's friend used to call her Lucy Locket after the children's nursery rhyme. As she grew up she maintained her childhood curiosity about lockets – she found the idea of them a very romantic notion and the thought of locks of hair or portraits handed down through generations as heirlooms was wonderful to her. Her interest sparked the idea of researching the origins of the locket as she found the whole history of such a meaningful trinket to be fascinating.

Her research spanned several years and was carried out as a hobby much in the way people research their family tree. Her hobby filled many lonely nights when she left her parent's home to move into a place of her own once she'd started work. Growing up, she had never been drawn to any career in particular and didn't really hold much fondness for the cut and thrust world of commerce and bustle of the modern working arena.

On leaving school she had fallen into different office jobs which made her feel empty and she yearned to be paid for something which she would enjoy. It was by chance that she discovered an advert for a vacancy at the museum in town in a discarded old newspaper she had, distractedly, picked up to browse whilst waiting for her turn in the chair at the hairdresser's.

Lisa had taken a picture of the advert on her mobile phone then rang them the second she emerged from the salon. The rest, as they say, was literally history! In her role at the museum Lisa was able to indulge her hobby whilst "working" at the same time as she began to familiarize herself with the objects on display and learned about their history in order to impart her knowledge to visitors to the museum.

She discovered that the existence of lockets dated back to the 16th century in European history. In this time, small lockets were worn as amulets to ward off evil spirits and would contain good luck charms. Other lockets, in this period, would contain a small piece of cloth soaked in sweet smelling perfume to defend against the stench of collective living in more densely packed areas. Small portraits were often placed in lockets to be passed on to an object of affection, too, which Lisa loved the idea of.

She found, though, that lockets were used in a more disturbing way in 1740. Lisa was sad to discover that locket necklaces were used to identify babies born to unmarried women in England. Children who were illegitimate suffered a tremendous social stigma. As a result, many of these unwed mothers ("fallen women") delivered their babies to foundling hospitals. The identical leaves of the locket necklace they were issued with were then separated. If a mother returned to claim her baby, she proved her maternity by presenting her half of the locket necklace and could reclaim her child. Lisa discovered this fact about lockets, by accident, when she watched a West End production of Annie during a shopping trip into London with her sister.

They had booked a "Theatre Package" weekend as a special early Christmas treat for themselves. Lisa had loved the bright lights and whole ambience of the theatre that night but the show, for her, was stolen by the moment that kidnappers posed as Annie's parents by presenting half of a locket necklace. She was shocked to learn of a darker use for the article of jewellery which she had always loved and always thought to be a gift of love.

Her sister, Karen, had enjoyed the show too but hadn't found it as poignant as Lisa and had been keen to go to get something to eat as soon as the curtain came down. Though the sky was dark when they emerged from the theatre the streets were still bright with the many lights from window displays and street lighting. They chose to eat in a small Italian restaurant just round the corner from their hotel and followed a route which took them through a Christmas market full of wooden cabins displaying their festive wares.

The air was filled with the smell of pine and mulled wine and, despite Karen's hunger, they took their time meandering through the little wooden huts. Karen stopped to buy a very delicate glass tree decoration for herself as she had just moved in with her boyfriend and she wanted to add her own personal touch to the place for their first Christmas living together as a couple.

She also found, on a nearby stall, a carved wooden nativity scene which she persuaded Lisa to put money towards to help her afford it for the "perfect spot on the table in the entranceway". Lisa, on the other hand, could find nothing of interest for herself. Everything was shiny and new and she preferred old things – she loved anything with a bit of history to it and she often thought she may have been born in the wrong century because she was so drawn to everything from by-gone eras.

Her favourite Christmas present, the previous year, had been a book from her mum and dad. They had presented her with a dog-eared antique copy of Jane Austen's *Sense and Sensibility* and Lisa had been thrilled to discover that a lock of hair in a locket was referenced to as a marriage proposal in the plot and, following this, further research in to the history of the locket also showed that using lockets to stash locks of hair had been used in more recent times as young soldiers, during World War One, would present their sweethearts with them before shipping out to various entrenched fronts.

Lisa loved classical literature and, often, browsed round antique shops and charity shops in the hope of finding a hidden gem. She became well-known to the shop owners and many of them would keep an eye out for anything which may be of interest for her. In this way she had recently bought an old edition of Emily Bronte's *Wuthering Heights* from the friendly owner of her favourite antique shop – Past Times.

She had devoured this classic over the space of a few nights as she made a habit of reading at bedtime. This was the part of the day she looked forward to the most and she had even bought a billowing old white, cotton nightgown which was part of a donation of costumes and props from the local amateur dramatic society at her favourite charity shop.

Lisa would don the old-fashioned nightgown and slide under the very modern duvet to travel back in time with a story in an old book which she often pondered the origins of as well – she would look at the beaten up old book fronts for a little while, some nights, and wonder who had picked up this book before her to read the story she was about to.

She also had an unusual ritual she used when she was reading an old book like this – she would remove her Laura Ashley bedside lamp and light a candle on her bedside table to read it by candlelight instead to help her immerse herself in the words of the past. Creating this ambience enabled her to imagine that she had journeyed back in time and it allowed her to feel that she became part of the story as she read on.

She had become so engrossed with the tumultuous love affair within the cover of *Wuthering Heights* that she could feel every wild gust of the moors as she read and hear the voices of the characters as the story unfolded before her in the soft, flickering glow of the candle. She had already concluded that this book was her all-time favourite well before reading about a scene where, at the death of Catherine, Heathcliff removed his rival-in-love Edgar's hair from her locket necklace and replaced it with his own to ensure that he was the one to be held close to her heart even in death.

Lisa could find nothing on the Christmas market that captured her imagination or sang to her heart more than this, recently read, book had done and she entered the Italian restaurant without any shopping bags apart from the ones she was helping Karen with. They ended a very enjoyable night with a filling bowl of pasta and retired, exhausted but happy, to their hotel to prepare for their return home the following day.

They were both tired and weary from the busy weekend and Karen and Lisa passed most of the train journey home in silence. Karen reviewed the contents of her shopping bags making mental notes of the best placing for each item and how she would wrap each of the gifts she had bought for her family whilst Lisa's thoughts drifted off to Emily Bronte's moors beyond Haworth and pondered what Christmas would have been like for Emily and her family at The Parsonage out in the wilds of Yorkshire in the height of winter.

Then her thoughts moved on to imagining what this Christmas would be like, for her, and how different it would be now that she had met the love of her life. The staff at the museum where Lisa worked were more like family than colleagues and Lisa had, instantly, felt welcomed into the fold when she turned up for an interview for the job in January that year. She hadn't met everyone on that first visit but found that the other, like-minded, people who worked there were all very friendly and welcoming too.

One of the people she met on her first day was Mike and, she smiled to herself at the memory that, it had been love at first lunchtime! Lisa and Mike had so much in common that both of them had forgotten to eat during that first lunchtime meeting and Lisa discovered that Mike worked, mainly, on the lower floor in the basement of the grand old building in the World Wars display. He spent his days making sure that the tape of the air raid sounded out loudly, and at regular intervals, to enhance the visitor's experience as they wound their way through the museum's version of a trench network in semi darkness.

Lisa had been assigned to the museum's tribute to the 19th Century era with its many artefacts and depictions of Queen Victoria's reign. As they only met up at lunchtime their relationship developed slowly but steadily over the weeks and months since Lisa's employment began at the museum and they eventually, and everyone thought inevitably, became a couple. Their weekends would involve going to various historic reenactments, antique fairs or just visiting castles or nearby cities with an eye out for architectural evidence of past occupants.

    When the train had arrived at the platform of their home town in Carnforth Lisa couldn't resist a quick look in at the Brief Encounter display whilst Karen ordered a reviving pot of tea and a scone each for them at the platform café before they parted ways. Though they were both tired from their long journey home they had decided to share a quick drink and something to "put them on", as their grandmother used to say, before continuing home.

Although Karen wasn't a history buff like her sister even she liked the thought that the film Brief Encounter had been made at their train station and thought it still felt like a romantic setting. When both she and Lisa had drained the teapot and finished off their scones Karen phoned her boyfriend to ask him to pick her up at the station for her own "brief encounter moment" and Lisa hugged her goodbye and left, with the promise to call later, to rescue her car from the snow-covered car park nearby.

When Christmas Day arrived both Lisa and Karen had designed a new Christmas tradition for their new relationship situations and Karen had been first to come up with a solution to the "who do we go to for Christmas Day?" dilemma. She had proposed a plan which would mean spending Christmas morning with her boyfriend at their flat then she would drive over to her parent's house for Christmas dinner where her boyfriend would join her later after visiting his parents.

This plan met with her parent's approval so, on the back of this, Lisa decided to spend Christmas morning on her own at her place then join Karen and her parents for Christmas dinner and Mike would join them all later that night. Now, though, as a frosty Christmas Day sunshine streamed through the thin curtains in Lisa's bedroom she was reluctant to throw the duvet back onto the coldness of the room so she left it to the last minute before a quick hot shower and wardrobe change.

She had skipped breakfast completely – safe in the knowledge that she would be eating plenty later. Dressed in sturdy boots (for the snow), a chunky cable jumper (for the cold) and carrying an armful of gifts (for Mick and her family) she braced herself for the brief cold walk to her car and the long moments of driving until the heater started to warm up. Before turning the ignition on she checked her mobile for messages and responded to a "Merry Christmas, love you! Can't wait to give you your present xx." message from Mike echoing his sentiments.

The path at her parents' house was lit with a chain of light-up snowmen which her mother had bought and forced her father to install for the day. The door was barely visible beneath the huge wreath of holly and red bows and the doorbell's regular chime had been replaced by one that played Silent Night in a warbling tone. Their mother did not "do Christmas" with her usual style and sophistication.

Silent Night alerted her dad to her arrival and she was soon in the warm embrace of her family in front of a roaring fire. This was the perfect Christmas scene that Lisa loved which evoked memories of childhood Christmases with a pillowcase of presents underneath the tree. The turkey dinner, as always, tasted as good as it smelt and Lisa felt warm and happy as she sat watching Karen's attempt to mime the latest film in the annual game of charades. Karen's boyfriend had arrived and had fitted, seamlessly, into the family celebrations with his enactment of the challenging title – *Gone With the Wind*. Then Silent Night warbled to announce the arrival of Mike and she eagerly ran to let him in.

It seemed odd, she thought, that Mike's arrival stopped the merrymaking. Charades ended abruptly with her dad's announcement of "right are we ready everyone?" Presents were exchanged and Lisa hadn't noticed that her mum had gone round the lounge lighting candles during the frenzy. Then her father addressed Mike and said "Right, son, on you go!" as he switched off the lights so that the room was lit only by candlelight and the glow from the fire.

Mike turned to Lisa and presented her with a small package which she opened slowly and carefully. She lifted the lid of the small box inside and had to wipe away a tear as she found a large, oval, antique locket inside. She was dazzled by its beauty and the fact that Mike had known the perfect thing to give her – Lucy Locket finally had a locket of her own! Then she opened it up to find a small note in each half of the frame – the first side read "Will you" and the second half read "Marry me?"

∞ ∞ ∞

Chapter Two.

A Christmas Angel?

Melissa had found herself in the only accommodation she could afford, following an expensive divorce, with her two young children. They moved into a cold, damp, unwelcoming old stone farm house which had been badly converted into two semi-detached dwellings. Apart from the adjoining neighbours there were no people for miles around and the lack of street lights made for an eerie dark silence after sunset.

The family of three made the best of their new surroundings by exploring the fields and woods with their Labrador until the winter weather forced them to stay indoors. As the nights drew in and the gas tank ran low Melissa kept up her own spirits and stayed positive for the children by baking cookies and making "real" hot chocolate on the stove. She held camp in the lounge where they would all huddle in a sleeping bag each with their baked goods and creamy chocolate drinks to watch Christmas movies on the television.

At weekends they would work together on various craft projects to make their new home look more festive and to make gifts in time for Christmas. The seasons were more noticeable in the countryside and they befriended a local gamekeeper who, much to Melissa's son's delight, imparted his wisdom each time he passed their way.

They had learned how to predict weather from nature and knew that the early crop of blackberries in the thick brambles in the hedgerows surrounding the fields predicted a cold hard winter. This was, apparently, nature's way of providing for the little creatures ready for the tough time ahead for them.

Melissa had harvested as many as she could and bought an old jam pan for 50p in a charity shop to make jams to bulk up their Christmas gift parcels for family and friends.

This also presented an enterprising opportunity for Melissa as her jams and chutneys proved to be very popular amongst her friends.

Melissa bought a large clear plastic "under bed storage box" and the children painted a sign saying "jam for sale" then they set up stall on their front wall. The narrow old lane was popular with walkers and cyclists and the majority of people who took jam, marmalade or chutneys used the honesty box honestly which gave Melissa enough to buy a nice Christmas present each for the children.

Along with Jim, the gamekeeper, another good friend was Geoff the postman who always had a chat on his rounds if he had time to stop. Melissa, as she had always done from the moment she had moved into her own place from her parents' house back in Yorkshire, had made a habit of baking Christmas cookies, mince pies and mini Christmas cakes for the postman, dustbin men, window cleaner (back in the day when she could afford one) and any neighbours. Her ex had called her pathetic for doing so but Melissa ignored him and did it anyway.

Geoff was partial to the mince pies and she used pretty ribbon to tie round clear bags to make them look more gift-like and festive. Nobody ever gave her the impression that her offerings were "pathetic" and they were always warmly received by anyone she bestowed them upon.

Moving to the new area meant that Melissa didn't have as many gifts to give that year but she still made something for the dustbin men (both regular refuse and the recycling team), Jim the gamekeeper and Geoff the postman along with the young couple next door who were rarely seen as they worked long hours at a farm at the end of the long lane.

Without realizing it, this small act of giving had earned Melissa a place in everyone's heart over the years and continuing this Christmas tradition helped her to feel more settled in the new area.

Although they made the best of the mouldy, draughty accommodation Melissa knew that it was no place to bring up young children as they constantly had chest infections and colds. She longed to be able to provide food and warmth for her children and felt like a failure for not being able to do so. Since the divorce, she had had to give up her business and auction off their home to pay her ex-husband's demands and cover the legal fees.

The divorce valued their old house and made the divorce settlement based on that value but, by the time the divorce was complete and Melissa was free to get rid of the house which held nothing but bad memories, the housing market had crashed leaving the house worth less than half the amount of its earlier valuation. Nobody was buying or selling and, as she could not afford to continue to live there, she had taken the only option open to her and sold the house at auction which left just enough to pay off the mortgage, the solicitors and replace the money in her children's savings accounts which her ex had taken from them.

She was penniless but, ever the optimist, she counted her blessings because the previous year had seen their home nearly repossessed at Christmas, when her ex moved out and stopped paying the mortgage, so at least they had a roof over their heads that year. Still she wanted a better future for her family and mentioned as much, in passing, to Geoff during the following autumn as another harsh winter threatened.

Geoff often popped in for a coffee and a slice of whatever had just been made and he got to know Melissa and her children well. He loved to share news of his wife, of whom he was immensely proud, and his two grown up children. As postmen know everything about village life, Melissa discovered, Geoff told her that a new development of affordable housing was due to be built in the following spring and suggested she should look into it to see if they were reserving them.

Having taken Geoff's advice, Melissa received a phone call on Christmas Eve to tell her that she would be able to move her family into one of the new homes in May. The rent was lower, they would have double glazing, insulation and heating and would be in the centre of the village with street lighting and wider roads to boot! This, also, meant that Geoff would still be their postie too – the children were thrilled.

Christmas was a happy time that year with thoughts of what the children might like their new bedrooms to look like and plans for the future. They started to pack up their belongings and make trips to the animal shelter charity shop with anything which would not be needed in their new home.

Having moved into a brand new house a few short months later, the three of them spent spring and summer upcycling junk shop furniture to make their home as cosy and welcoming as they could afford. When the winter set in they didn't need to watch television in a sleeping bag anymore and they excitedly prepared for their first Christmas in their new warm, dry home.

They even bought a new artificial Christmas tree as the mice had eaten their old one at the old house. Everything was twinkly and perfect until one morning's school run the car, which was older than the children, seemed to, finally, lose the will to live. Their friendly new neighbour gave the children a lift into school on her way to work while Melissa pondered what to do and worried about the expense.

As she stood, as if frozen, on the driveway Geoff arrived to drop off the latest batch of Christmas cards for her and asked what she was doing outside on such an icy cold morning. It turned out, after she'd explained the situation, that he knew of a "really decent bloke just down the road with a garage that looks like a scrap yard".

Melissa called the mobile number which Geoff had given her before he headed on up the street to make the rest of his deliveries. She explained to the "decent bloke" on the other end of the line that Geoff the postman had given her his number and suggested she called him. After hearing Melissa's explanation about what had happened shortly before her car refused to budge Chris offered to walk down and take a look to see if he could coax it back to life for her.

Stood in the cold, watching out for the mechanic, Melissa couldn't believe her eyes as Chris turned the corner - he was very handsome! As she shook his extended hand to introduce herself and felt tingles at his touch, Melissa pondered the possibility that maybe Geoff the postman was actually really a Christmas Angel in Royal Mail disguise!

∞ ∞ ∞

Chapter Three

An Unforgettable Christmas.

Karl had been Carol's husband for longer than she cared to remember and she looked across at him snoring next to her in the passenger seat and thought to herself how far they'd come since they had found each other against all odds. Fate, serendipity – whatever it was, Carol felt blessed that she had found her soulmate. Karl continued to snore but turned, in his sleep, to face her with a smile on his face and Carol wondered what must be going through his mind.

There could have been so many ways that their lives could've gone & every opportunity for their paths never to have crossed at all. Karl had moved to Swansea to move back in with his parents after realizing that life in the RAF was not for him and, to raise money, he sold his car so that he could go into business with his younger brother, Stuart. After selling his Peugeot at auction Karl had no idea that the mechanic from Preston, who had snapped up the bargain, would go on to sell it to Carol miles away. Carol had had no idea what buying this car would lead her to or the journey the car would take her on both physically and metaphorically speaking.

Bored and lonely, one day, Carol had impulsively decided to have a "run out" in the car for the day and had heard of a craft fair that was on several miles away in Skipton. Being small she had always struggled to see over the top of the car doors or reach the roof when she was washing it. She had just loaded up the car with her essentials for the journey a new mix CD, her handbag, mobile phone and coffee in a travel mug.

She misjudged the angle as she reached across the driver's seat and spilled coffee into the holder, on the car seat and burned her hand slightly. Her reflex reaction was to recoil, still with the cup of hot coffee in her hand, whilst swearing. As she shook the drips of coffee from her hands and tried to mop the damp patch which had appeared on her jeans, she was embarrassed to see that the postman had arrived and had witnessed and, more embarrassingly, heard everything.

To his credit the postman pretended he hadn't heard all of this and had offered a cheerful greeting whilst trying to pass a small stack of letters across to her over her car door (the driveway was narrow and the thick hedges at either side made passage by the car impossible).

As Carol couldn't reach over the door, she closed it and reached out for her letters as the sound of the car locking itself made them both jump. It turned out that the car had a mind of its own and would lock itself after a few seconds if it thought that nobody was getting in it. It must have thought that Carol had changed her mind and decided not to go out but had forgotten to lock the car before going back in the house.

Unfortunately it had done all of this with Carol's bag and phone inside but also, more importantly, the keys in the ignition. Not only was she locked out of the car but the house too. Luckily the postman had saved the day with a screwdriver and a length of break cable which he, worryingly, had to hand in the back of his van.

She didn't ask how he had acquired the skills he used to gain access to her car but assumed he must've been good at "hook-a-duck" as a kid and that he must have won lots of goldfish! Relieved and grateful, Carol changed her journey plans at his suggestion to get another key cut for the car in case it ever happened again in the future. So she pointed the car in the direction of the nearest key cutter's.

Emerging, disgruntled, some time later from the cobbler's which offered a key cutting service she reminisced that her grandad would have remarked that the cobbler "should have been wearing a mask and cape at those prices – daylight robbery!" Carol had, as her grandad would have done, walked out of the shop without a spare key.

Not knowing where to go or what to do to get a key which was affordable, Carol drove over to the garage where she had bought the car to ask if they might have been given a spare with it when they got it. They hadn't but suggested she look on the car's log book because it would have the details of the previous owner on there and she might be able to contact them to see if they might still have one that they could send her.

Not hopeful she decided that the cost of a phone call to enquire was worth it as the garage had told her that the price the Cobblers' had suggested was competitive. Carol returned home and found the paperwork with Karl's address on it and the internet provided a phone number for the address so, as long as Karl was still at the same address, she would be able to get in touch.

Having felt nervous ringing a complete stranger it had taken several cups of coffee and a bit of pacing up and down before Carol had plucked up courage to dial the number to ask a stranger for help. Two hours later she had bid farewell to Karl and felt like they had known each other all of their lives.

It didn't seem strange or concerning at all, to her, that she had agreed to travel down to Wales at the weekend to meet Karl who had confirmed that he did have a spare key because he had loved the car and had been loathed to let it go. He felt, by keeping the key, he still held onto it a bit. They had both laughed on the phone when he had explained this and he realized how crazy this sounded when he said it out loud.

The long drive down to Swansea on a cold Saturday in December gave Carol a lot of singing time and she managed to work her way through every track on both discs of her *Now That's What I call Christmas* CD. When she had pulled up in front of Karl's parents' home she didn't feel wary or in any way scared; instead she felt more a sense of déjà vu somehow.

The long journey had meant that it was dark when she had turned into their street and she was thrilled to see that the whole street had decorated their homes with strings of Christmas lights, inflatable snowmen and various Santas lit up in their gardens. Carol had meticulously planned her journey using the AA AutoRoute and a stack of post-it-notes stuck across the dashboard, as was the way before the introduction of satnavs, but she hadn't factored in the fact that the daylight hours were shorter at this time of year and, though it wasn't really late, the sky was dark enough to show off the twinkling Christmas lights to best effect.

Carol had tried to knock on the door but nobody came and she could hear sound through the window alongside the door so she had moved across the path and raised her hand to tap on the window but had paused at the sight of Karl.

He was just reaching down to pass his mum a cup of tea and she noticed that he was wearing an elf jumper. That was the moment she had fallen for him! She decided that anybody who would wear an elf jumper must have a sense of humour or, at least, a sense of duty to wear it to please his folks. That first impression had told Carol everything she needed to know about the man. It confirmed what she had felt during their lengthy phone conversation – that he must be a kind and caring man.

When Carol had been welcomed inside, the attraction between herself and Karl was immediate and she stayed and chatted with him, his parents and his brother until she lost track of time. She had been invited to share a meal with them before the long journey back which she had accepted gratefully.

When it came time to leave she said goodbye to everyone who had assembled in the hallway to bid her farewell then she had turned to open the door to a blizzard and a large pile of snow which fell onto the doormat from where it had drifted up against the front door since she had arrived.

Karl's mum had insisted she couldn't go out on a night like that and had insisted she stay the night. Carol had been kitted out with one of Karl's mum's winceyette nighties and a hot water bottle and Karl had opted to sleep on the settee so that she could have his room. They made her feel very at home and she had been glad to be able to spend longer in their company.

Since their wedding two years after that meeting, Karl and Carol had been inseparable and Karl moved up to join her in Lancashire. He had spent time working alongside Stuart in their plumbing business until the move and he had made enough money to be able to start up on his own in his new hometown. They had spent many long and happy years together and felt completely at ease with each other. They knew everything about each other and Carol felt that Karl's family regarded her as the daughter they had never had.

They had been shocked to hear the news which Carol had had to impart just a few days before this year's latest migration back to Swansea for Christmas. She hadn't known how to break it to them and she hadn't fully digested what she had learned herself at that stage either. But, at the sound of her mother-in-law's voice when she picked the phone up the words had come to her in a flurry.

Karl was still asleep as Carol pulled into the service station just past Birmingham. She turned the engine off and the combination of the engine sound and the CD player stopping with the bright lights emitted from the service station entrance woke Karl up. He had smiled sleepily across at Carol and, for a split second, she had melted inside before reminding herself what this man alongside her had done and the fact that, after all these years, he was a stranger to her now.

She had asked Karl to go into the services for a coffee and a sausage roll for them both to sustain them for the remainder of the journey while she used the toilets but had doubled back to the car once he was out of sight. She flicked the central locking button on the key fob and quickly removed his suitcase from the boot of the car. Carol deposited the case up against the kerb in a puddle of slush then jumped into the car and pressed send on the pre-typed text she had prepared to notify the woman that she had discovered Karl had been having an affair with that he needed collecting from Moto Frankley service station.

Karl's mother had been disgusted to hear about the affair and had lamented that her son had always strayed in every relationship before he had met Carol and confessed that she had hoped he would have changed his ways when he had met "the one". His brother, Stuart, had wanted to, immediately, drive up to Lancashire to leap to Carol's defense but his father had prevented him from doing something rash and suggested that Carol should go down, on her own, to see them for Christmas as she had every year since that first snowy Christmas for the spare key for them all to discuss it and decide what was best to do.

Carol had been overcome with emotion to feel so loved by a family who, technically, weren't hers and had not trusted herself to confront Karl because she knew that he would insist she was mistaken and try to placate her whilst convincing her she was paranoid. Instead, she carried out the plan she had formulated with Karl's family. She turned the ignition and the old favourite Christmas CD sprung into life, aptly she thought, with Chris Rea's Driving Home for Christmas as she pointed the car towards her future – leaving the past behind.

∞ ∞ ∞

Chapter Four

Christmas Miracle.

My last delivery of the day was also my favourite and I looked forward to the welcome that awaited me behind the steamy windows of the Poppins Tearoom in Taunton. The tinkle of the cheery bell above the door as I entered always made me feel like I had reached the finish line of my own personal marathon. Since I'd taken on the floundering family business, following my dad's heart attack and subsequent recuperation, I had begun to realise just how hard dad had worked all those years while I went to university in a bid to become a vet. Little did I know that no matter how hard I tried I would never get away from the farm.

Although my dad was convinced that cider was the only way forward, the downturn in business over the years indicated otherwise. I had not wanted to worry him about the figures and what they meant for the future of the farm. I had kept my concerns to myself when I had taken a look at the accounts when mum asked me to fill my dad's wellies, so to speak, and take over the family business. We both knew that dad would never be the rough and ready, 'hands like shovels', action man he had always been – bossing everyone around at harvest time. Taking over from dad would not be a temporary measure. My plans for the future had to change. My years of study would not lead to a veterinary practise as I had hoped.

I had joined the local Young Farmers group where I met and, later, married the girl of my dreams. Sharon had been the only girl for me and, despite my attempts to be a ladies man during my university years, I was utterly besotted as soon as we locked eyes at the Harvest Ball in Wellington. We were married with my dad as my best man. He had looked so proud and touched when I'd asked him to do the honours and had accepted eagerly.

His best man speech didn't leave a dry eye in the house when he acknowledged that I had sacrificed my hopes of becoming a vet to take over the cider farm which he was proud to hand down to me and was, now, looking forward to me passing it on to future generations. I still didn't have the heart to tell him just how bad things were financially and it was a very real prospect that the land may have to be sold to property developers to stop the farm from being repossessed. Only Sharon shared my knowledge and concerns regarding the business. I did not and could not possess the depth of knowledge that my dad had acquired over the years about the crops, the process, the flavours and acidity that culminated in the sweet golden liquid which was synonymous with our family name. But I knew that I would be the last generation to farm the land if I didn't find a way to diversify.

The early days of our marriage had been busy, exhausting and fraught with anxiety about our family home and income and my dad's frail health. It had never occurred to either of us that we may not be able to have children. The assumption amongst the farming community was that you got married and started a brood within a year – sadly this wasn't to be for Sharon and me.

In a cruel twist of irony, Mother Nature had deemed that I would be the last generation of my family to farm the land even if Sharon and I did manage to turn the business around. After being told at the 20 week scan that our baby was not developing properly and could not survive the "gross foetal abnormalities" we were told that we had no option but to induce labour rather than go full term and deliver our baby stillborn. This was abhorrent to both of us but I had to insist that we followed the doctor's advice when he told us that there were health implications for Sharon to continue with the pregnancy.

The pain and anguish of the weeks that followed affected us both deeply and I tried to be stoic about everything and tried to be strong for both of us. Sharon was, understandably, in bits and she mistook my chipper front and unwillingness to talk about what had happened as me not caring.

To say the subsequent years were a difficult patch of our marriage is an understatement and our lives were barren in many respects. The only positive thing to come out of this hideous twist of fate was that we both threw ourselves into making the business work as neither of us slept well after the loss of our baby and the revelation that we might never have children.

As we hardly slept and kept busy, during our waking hours, to keep our minds off our bitter disappointment and grief we had very long working days which were filled with maintaining the cider production whilst exploring other avenues to diversify into other more lucrative areas which could then subsidise the farming side of our business. Sharon came up with one of our most successful and enduring ideas to make a bit of extra cash on the side one windy late September afternoon as she walked through the orchard back to the house.

She noticed just how many apples had fallen to the ground as the heavily laden branches could not shield their fruit from the winds that rattled through the rows of twisted tree trunks and gnarly branches.

The movement of the unyielding thick branches in the wind meant that the heaviest and ripest apples easily snapped away and fell to the ground to rot or be eaten by passing wildlife. Sharon commented, on her return, what a waste it was for so many of our apples to just fall and rot like that when they could easily be put to use somehow if we collected them in as soon as they fell.

So, twenty years on, there I was still delivering our windfall apples around the local shops and cafes who bought them from us at a cheaper rate than they could from their regular produce suppliers because some of the apples would need to be cut away which left less of the actual fruit that could be used. We crated them up with this in mind so the loss in quality was made up for in quantity and our regular customers were quite happy to do a bit of extra preparation for the savings they made and the superior quality of our flavours.

This had, indeed, proved to be quite a successful venture albeit a very seasonal one. The money we raised from doing this in the autumn time had helped us through many a cold winter over the years and as word of mouth spread across the area our deliveries had increased. Sharon had started her own "James' Farm Homemade Pies" company which sold frozen apple pies to supermarkets throughout Somerset as the years passed and her farm shop expanded into a small scale manufacturing set-up in one of the renovated barns at the back of the farm.

I took care of the deliveries and I always saved my favourite delivery till last. Ruth the rotund, ruddy-cheeked proprietor of Poppins Tearoom was our best customer and she always proffered a warming pot of tea tucked under a hand knitted cosy and a slice of pie for me to reward me at the end of my rounds. One particularly wet September afternoon I was surprised to see that the café was completely full which was unusual. My favourite table, which was always available on my Friday afternoon visits usually, was occupied by a young girl who Ruth informed me had been "sat there for ages with a milkshake and a face that looked like it could curdle it."

A brief look around had confirmed that all of the other tables were full, even the three round the corner behind the coat stand and overgrown umbrella plant. Ruth informed me that her usual custom had been swelled to capacity by a surge of visitors to an event called the Wellington Game Fair & Horse Trials – a snooty affair that didn't hit my radar of interest in the slightest but which obviously proved to be popular with others.

I decided to approach the angry looking young girl who did not look like one of the horsey types. My day had been long and tiring - it had only been tolerable in the knowledge that at the end of my rounds would be a sit down, a catch up on the local gossip, a reviving cuppa and a warm piece of Ruth's apple pie as a reward for my efforts. I did not feel that I could miss out on my prize for a hard day's work because a bunch of townies had descended on us for the weekend.

I reached my favourite table and smiled at its occupant who glowered at me in return. Unperturbed I stretched out my hand and, by way of introduction, announced my name closely followed by "mind if I join you?" and then sat down as my request was met with a shrug which I interpreted as affirmation or, if not, just indifference and I took up my position at the table. The young girl had looked disgusted but didn't say anything and just continued to stare into her milkshake.

I had felt the silence very awkward and had tried to make conversation with "You off school today?" but she just ignored me and I felt really uncomfortable and had regretted choosing to sit there. I had been, momentarily, spared the awkward silence as my pot of tea and sweet-smelling pie had been placed before me but I instinctively knew that this young child needed it more than me and I had pushed the bowl across to the her and nodded that she eat it.

Still – she had remained silent but had devoured the pie as if it was the first bite of food she'd had for some time and I gently enquired if she lived nearby or was just visiting for the horse show. I was shocked that, her response had been to release a big tear which dripped into her empty bowl. Not one at ease with my own emotions, never mind anyone else's, I had been lost for words and had just sat staring at the poor child whilst desperately searching for the right thing to say. Something which Sharon had assured me, on many occasions, I was rubbish at.

The child had wiped her runny nose across her sleeve then pulled the cuffs of her cardigan down over her hands and used them to dry her eyes then she looked at me, thanked me and scraped her chair backwards as if to leave. A rush of protectiveness washed over me in that instant and I knew that I couldn't let this young girl walk out alone to who knows what or where. The only thing I managed to come up with was to say "that pie is made by the apples from my farm and my wife, Sharon, makes pies too in the barn. Would you like to come and meet her and take a few more pies home with you?"

Rightly, the child looked wary and I realised that I was a stranger trying to lure a child into my van – a scenario that every parent, teacher and responsible adult warned against but my heart had gone out to her and I wanted to keep her safe. Something inside me just knew that something was wrong and I believed she was running away from something. To reassure her I had suggested we telephone her mum to ask if it would be ok for her to visit the farm but she told me that her mum was dead which stunned me back into silence.

The tears had begun to flow freely as she continued to share that her mum had died in the early hours of that morning and the child, I now knew to be Claudia, had fled from home when her step father woke her to break the news that her mother had been killed in a car accident by a drunk driver as she was making her way home from working a night shift in her role as a respiratory nurse at Taunton's Musgrove Park Hospital.

Her step-father had been unkind to her and her mother so, on hearing the tragic news, she had taken every penny out of her piggy bank, sneaked out of the house and got a bus then another and another until her piggy bank savings had gone and she'd found herself in our sleepy little village in Poppins Tearoom. It sounded like Rosie had also felt protective towards the child and given her a free milkshake when she had entered the tearoom, claiming that on Fridays the first child to walk in won a free milkshake.

The child had taken her "prize" and hidden in my favourite seat where she could hide away but still see everything that was going on. I favoured that spot for the same reason I realised, that day, as I gathered up my coat and nodded my thanks to Rosie then told Claudia that we would both go and explain everything to Sharon who would know what to do and would sort everything out as she always did.

We had both pulled our coats tighter against us as we left the warmth of the tearoom and ventured into the rain and, as I pointed towards the van something caught my eye. It was a black and white kitten that was bedraggled and looked so forlorn that I bent and scooped it up to share some warmth. Claudia told me that the kitten had followed her from the bus stop at the other end of the village as if she was lost and, after a quick examination of the poor thing I realised that she showed signs of upper respiratory problems probably because she was way too young to be out and probably hadn't had any injections.

I explained to Claudia that Moggy, as Claudia had named her, must be a stray and she was a little bit poorly but, as a vet, I knew we could make her all better with a bit of medicine, lots of fluids and lots of rest. Then Claudia cuddled Moggy to keep her warm on the journey back to the farm where Sharon was surprised, to say the least, when I turned up with a little girl and a kitten but, as always, she knew just what to do and how to fix everything. I fixed Moggy while Sharon gave Claudia a change of clothes then warmed her by the fire in the kitchen with a cup of hot chocolate while she made a few phone calls.

That was to mark a very big change in our lives as we made plans to reutilise an abandoned outhouse as a rescue centre for sick, injured or homeless animals. We were going through the process of adopting Claudia too and Sharon had always been a capable, strong woman but at the start of December she started to get tired really easily which we both put down to the stress of all the changes and everything involved to bring the changes about. Her brothers, Ben, Tom and Joe had all come to lend a hand with the building work which was a huge help to us.

Things were all coming together but it was a lot to handle all at once and I was worried that Sharon was overdoing things when, just a couple of days before Christmas, she fainted in the kitchen and then confessed that she'd been feeling a little off-colour for a while and had been constantly nauseous and, occasionally, had been sick. She had reluctantly visited the Doctor the day before Christmas Eve and reported back that the Doctor said it was nothing to worry about.

Relieved that she was ok and distracted with the rescue centre plans I didn't put two and two together as you'd expect anybody with any medical inclination might do so I was stunned when I opened my Christmas card from Sharon on Christmas day and read "Nappy Christmas, love. Next year Claudia will have a little brother or sister!"

∞ ∞ ∞

Chapter Five

Away With a Stranger!

Marian and Brenda were neighbours and, over the years, had grown to share a deep friendship as well as a fence. They had shared many things in the time they had spent living next to each other. Their children had played out together on the road in front of their houses and had each moved away to live, work or study as independent adults within the space of a three year period. Marian and Brenda had helped each other through the teenage tantrum turmoils then the empty nest stage and, more recently, the death of their husbands.

The trials that life had given them made them both stronger individually and also strengthened their bond of friendship. They knew that, whatever happened, they would always have each other and they both took comfort in that knowledge. Each year they would go away for Christmas "so as not to be a burden on anybody" on a Tinsel and Turkey Coach Trip.

This became their Christmas tradition and, after several Christmases spent this way, they discovered that these trips were frequented by the same people in similar situations to themselves. They struck up a coach trip friendship group and Marian, being the younger of the two neighbours and therefore more "tech savvy" as she put it, took it upon herself to take down everybody's phone numbers of the Tinsel and Turkey regulars and set up a WhatsApp group for them all to communicate from their far-flung corners of England, Scotland, Ireland and Wales in order to make arrangements to ensure that they were all able to congregate at the same hotel together in the forthcoming years.

A sociable sort, as Marian was, she had flitted from table to table in the dining room of the previous year's hotel "mingling and circulating", as she phrased it, to ascertain who wanted to be part of the "TnT" group she was setting up for the following year. It was at one of these tables that she stayed and chatted longer than she had at the other tables which she had landed on and fluttered away with names and numbers like a butterfly.

She 'landed' at the table where a gentleman sat alone with his after dinner coffee and wafer mint. Marian hadn't seen him before and had introduced herself, informed him of her mission and then fell into easy conversation with him. Marian was a real 'people-person' with a warmth that radiated from her and drew people to her. The gentleman welcomed the conversation and her easy nature and they chatted for some time.

Brenda had noticed that Marian had been gone a long time and calculated that she must have had enough time to get round to everyone by now. She had gone off to find Marian, worried that she may have got lost somehow or, worse, she may have been accosted by a stranger. That was the only thing that Brenda didn't like about going away – the fact that the places you went to were filled with folk you didn't know and she had a distrust of anything or anyone that was unfamiliar to her. She was a creature of routine and habit.

To her, her concern for Marian was real and, in the few paces she had made from their table in the candlelit dining room with its huge Christmas tree dropping pine needles everywhere, she had managed to convince herself that Marian must have fallen foul to the evil clutches of one of the dodgy-looking waiters that had served them. She'd warned Marian not to wear her string of pearls for fear of attracting unsavoury types!

Brenda collided with Marian as she made her way to the foyer to raise the alarm for her missing friend. Marian had finished her conversation with the charming gentleman and had agreed to add his number to the group then had visited the Ladies' room which she was returning from when Brenda had literally run into her. They had returned to their table together and watched the entertainment which the hotel had laid on for them all then they retired to their rooms to prepare for bed and the long coach ride home after breakfast the following morning.

Brenda had already packed her case and had just left out her toiletries, night things and her outfit for travelling home in. Marian, however, who was in the room next door to Brenda thought that her room had been burgled when she opened her door before she realised that she had left it that way.

Marian, hurriedly, threw her belongings into her case after oversleeping slightly and was flustered, yet still packed and ready, by the time she reached the breakfast buffet. Thankfully, Brenda had ordered a pot of coffee for them both which she was grateful for. After a 'Full English' Brenda and Marian took up their favourite position at the front of the coach and Marian passed the journey back setting up everybody's details into her new 'TnT' group while Brenda enjoyed the scenery.

Marian sent her very first group WhatsApp message as soon as she'd put the kettle on when she got back home. She sent a general message hoping that everybody had enjoyed their Christmas as much as she had and wished everybody a Happy New Year.

The initial message from Marian had met with a flurry of responses from everyone in the group including the gentleman that had stayed on a Christmas coach-break for the first time. Her stomach did a little flip when she noticed messages from him and, soon, they had begun to communicate on a one-to-one basis outside of the group.

Life continued much the same apart from this and she continued to go round to Brenda's every couple of days to share a pot of tea and to share each other's news. Somehow, Marian didn't feel she could tell Brenda about her message swapping with the gentleman because she knew that Brenda wouldn't approve of her conducting herself in this way. So she kept it to herself.

The months passed and Brenda was content that everything was as it should be and all was in order. She raced round to

Marian's as soon as the coach company released their trip schedule for the winter months and festive season to plan where to go for the upcoming Tinsel and Turkey trip. Marian, at that point, was forced to explain that she wasn't sure whether she wanted to go or not.

Brenda, as expected, was shocked and couldn't understand this sudden and unsettling change so Marian took advantage of her shocked silence to rush into damage limitation mode and hurriedly explained that this wouldn't change their friendship and maybe it was time that Brenda accepted her family's invitations to spend Christmas with them. Brenda didn't take it well!

Several days passed without the neighbours convening for their usual brew and chat and both missed the other immensely. During this time Marian finalised her arrangements with her gentleman friend to spend Christmas abroad together in Turkey whilst Brenda couldn't decide what to do with herself. She couldn't decide whether to go on the coach trip by herself or whether to accept her daughter's invitation to stay with them from Christmas Eve through until New Year. She loved the idea of spending the festive period with her grandchildren but didn't want to feel like she was getting in the way and, truth be known, she liked her quiet ordered way of life and she knew that her daughter's home would be chaotic.

Marian plucked up courage and knocked on Brenda's door with a poinsettia plant. This was one of their traditions – whichever one of them spotted the first poinsettia in the supermarket would buy one for them both. Without children around their homes they had both discarded the idea of wrestling an artificial tree out of the loft to wrap it in lights and trim it with garish decorations just for the sake of a few days (and with them usually being away over Christmas it didn't seem worth bothering).

The poinsettia was the only nod to festivity which either of them indulged in and it was always a special moment when the plants landed on the shelves as it heralded the start of the season. Brenda opened the door to a huge poinsettia on legs which she knew to be Marian with a peace offering – she cried!

Several cups of tea later and half a box of tissues used between them the neighbours had shared their memories of Christmases past – their childhood memories of a sock filled with hazelnuts, their memories of taking their children to meet Father Christmas at Lewis's in Manchester and giving them tangerines in their stockings then the Christmases they had shared together once their families had outgrown the magic of it all.

Comforted by the thoughts of happy times and shared history, Brenda was reassured that spending this Christmas apart wouldn't spell the end of such a special and enduring friendship and they both hugged each other in a silent acknowledgment that, though that year things would be different, everything would be ok.

Brenda had waved goodbye to Marian until she couldn't see her taxi anymore as it sped towards the airport to meet her new travel companion. She was collected, soon after, by her daughter and taken back to her house where the children were baking in the kitchen with their dad who Brenda had always liked. The smell of cinnamon and ginger brought all of those happy memories flooding back again to Brenda and, though the children were both covered in flour and shrieking with laughter, Brenda instantly felt at home and wondered why she hadn't done this sooner.

She tucked the children in bed at the end of the night, as she had her own two, and read 'Twas The Night Before Christmas' to them as she always had on Christmas Eve when her children were little. Snuggled down for the night and one of them already asleep before she reached the end, Brenda tiptoed back downstairs to share grown up time with her daughter and son-in-law.

They had used the distraction of Grandma to sneak out the presents and set the scene with half eaten mince pies and carrots next to the chimney with an empty glass of sherry. They all finally sat down and raised a glass to a merry Christmas then her son-in-law had to ask "so where's Marian this year" to his wife's disapproval. She knew that this was still a sore point for her mum even though she had accepted the situation and she winced as her mum responded with "well son – she's away with a stranger and I'll tell you something! Might be Turkey but I bet you there'll be no ruddy tinsel!"

∞ ∞ ∞

Chapter Six

Sally's Secret Santa.

The office Christmas party was well under way and much merry was being made! Everyone had got into the festive spirit and seemed to all have morphed into their alter egos as they indulged in the free festive spirits from the open bar. The bosses were very generous and regarded their staff as their extended family. They thought that a boozy Christmas party was the best way to share the season of good will with everyone before they all went home to share their more intimate Christmas gatherings with their own families.

This annual Christmas event was the highlight of Bob's year and had been since he founded the company many years back. He had built up the business in his youth when he came up with the idea of selling personalised Secret Santa gifts. The idea of workplaces putting everyone's name into a hat to each be chosen by somebody (who had to keep their identity a secret from their recipient). This meant that each person only had to buy one gift and everyone received one. A good idea, in principal, but one which often proved difficult for everyone.

It was common to put a spending limit on the gift which was problematic because everybody had to aim to spend as near to the amount as possible. Also, larger offices with more employees meant that people often didn't know each other well enough to know what to get. For many, the buying of the Secret Santa gift was the hardest present to buy on their Christmas shopping list.

So The Secret Santa Shop was set up online with a range of gifts set at fixed prices such as £5 or £10 which seemed to be the most commonly requested on their website. Bob also, later, set up a special section of the online shop for personalised Secret Santa gifts which allowed a person to give details about the recipient for a tailor-made gift to be made especially for them.

Due to the early success of Bob's business he had, quickly, had to take on people to help him. He had advertised his job vacancies in his local post office and newspaper with the headline "Secret Santa needs elves to help out in the Christmas shop!" From this initial advert he managed to employ five elves who all loved him and the informal atmosphere of his office which was trimmed for Christmas all year round to keep him and his elves in the festive spirit all the time in order to focus their thoughts on sourcing suitable gifts and packaging for the next Christmas.

The six of them didn't feel like they were working because they all loved what they were doing and they would often arrive early and leave late because they couldn't stay away from the place without missing it. As the business continued to grow they had noticed a lot of enquiries asking for gifts to a set amount but for a theme or something special for that special someone and Bob took the decision to advertise for a Special Elf to join their family in order to put together the personalised gifts which they were struggling to create themselves.

This was how Bob met Sally! Sally had gone for her interview dressed in a suit and carrying a briefcase as she had done to every other interview she'd been to. However, on arrival, Bob met her at the reception desk, stored her briefcase behind Rose the elf's desk and gave her a Santa hat to put on while they walked through the office. This was Bob's way of choosing the right person for the job – If they refused the hat or laughed at him they would not fit in with his existing elves or his own company ethos.

Sally had not only eagerly put the hat on but had said that, if she'd known, she would have come in her own Christmas hat which lit up and said "ho, ho, ho" when a button was pressed. Bob knew, with certainty from that moment, that she was his Special Elf and he took her on the tour of the small office and then the packaging and distribution room where she was greeted by Olly and William who gave her a full run down of "Elf and Safety" guidelines in operation. She met two more elves then Bob took her to his office which was more of a grotto with all the tinsel, lights, baubles and huge artificial tree filling a corner of the room. Sally loved it!

After Sally's successful interview in July she began work straight away and travelled around local craft shops to find out what could be custom made and to negotiate deals to prepare for the forthcoming Christmas. When she wasn't travelling around sourcing unusual bespoke items she spent her time at the office where she had been given her own little desk in her own little room with her own huge artificial Christmas tree. She brought in a big notice board and William helped her to put it up on the larger of the walls behind her desk.

Rose supplied her with a pack of drawing pins and Sally began to create a Christmas "mood board" of gift ideas, packaging, ribbon and craft ideas. In this way she built a collection of gifts which she could put together to make the perfect personal present for anyone. Her go-to general gift for all, if she wasn't given a lot of detail about the recipient, would be a large heart shaped gingerbread biscuit which had a hole at the top and a red, gingham hanging ribbon threaded through. These were made by a very funny lady, called Toni, who she had met on her reconnaissance mission and had instantly gelled with. Toni could ice any name or message on to the biscuits in order to personalise them.

Bob changed the website to show the new personalised offering and Sally went out and about to offices and local businesses to tell them about the service they provided and to leave flyers with her business card. She also came up with the idea that if a company ordered all of their Secret Santa gifts through them, through the use of another button on the website which operated in a similar way to a wedding gift list, they could be personally delivered and distributed by an elf at their party or to their place of work.

Because of these innovations the business thrived and the weeks leading up to Sally's first Christmas in the job were chaotically busy but so enjoyable for all of the elves which now totalled fifteen. Business was so good that Bob had had to draft in extra help which included some of their suppliers who often stayed behind after dropping off a delivery to pitch in if they were needed.

As one of their most regular visitors was Toni, with her gingerbread hearts, and as she helped out so much they made her an honorary elf and presented her with her very own personalised Santa hat which had her name embroidered on the front (one of the personal gifts that Sally had managed to source).

Despite the run up to Christmas being their busiest time of the year Bob insisted, every year, that they all have a party on the night before Christmas Eve for him to thank them for their friendship, loyalty and hard work through the year. From humble beginnings, the gatherings grew from Bob buying everyone fish and chips from the local chip shop to the more recent grand affairs as the business grew along with his financial stability.

He was a creative soul and loved to surprise everyone with thoughtful treats and experiences. One year had seen them all partying on a barge down the canal and another year had seen him hiring out an old studio where Sherlock Holmes had been filmed and they all dined at big round tables on a cobbled street underneath artificial stars on a darkened set of Baker Street. Each year, he hired a coach to take them all from the office then made sure they each were deposited safely at their doors before going home himself.

All of the elves loved the suspense of what he would come up with each year and they had never been disappointed. Sally's personal favourite Christmas party was a masked ball which Bob had arranged in a huge ballroom with high ceilings and chandeliers at a stately home. He had kitted everyone out in Georgian costumes for the night and themed the night based on Sally's love for all things 'Pride and Prejudice' and he cast himself in the role of her favourite fictional character – Mr. Darcy.

Secretly, Bob had been planning his masked ball extravaganza for many months because it would also be the occasion where he proposed marriage to his Special Elf who had become his business partner. Their friendship had turned into a relationship and then a deep love for each other in the three years that Sally had worked there and he wanted to make her his partner in life as well as business. He couldn't think of any better way to propose to her than surrounded by the elves, who were their family, and at their favourite time of year.

With a great deal of effort on his part he had managed to put into place all the arrangements and managed to keep it a secret from everyone. As usual he had hired a Father Christmas, for the night, to distribute gifts to all of his staff. The sack of presents included a gift from him to everyone and then their own Secret Santa gifts for each other. All of the staff ate a meal together then danced until 10.30pm when Father Christmas arrived to hand out the parcels before "coaches at 11pm" to ensure that everyone was home safely with their nearest and dearest for Christmas.

This part was always the perfect end to a perfect night and everyone had gathered round the beautifully lit towering Christmas tree at the end of the ballroom that night. Only Sally had noticed that Bob was nowhere to be seen. She instinctively missed him if she didn't feel his presence by her side or if he wasn't in view and she had begun to feel anxious at his absence. Then, as Father Christmas slung his empty sack over his shoulder and made his way towards the door to a round of applause and cries of "Merry Christmas", Sally saw Bob out of the corner of her eye.

She turned to see him coming out from behind the tree and he addressed everyone once Father Christmas had left the room. He usually did a thank you speech to everyone at this point but this time his demeanor had a different feel and some of the female elves shared expectant glances between each other. Sally was transfixed as he spoke to the room but looked only at her as h everyone how much she meant invited her over to join him where he bended knee and asked her to make his happiest man in the world and allow him be her Mr. Darcy. She had agreed but said that she would "rather be known as Mrs. Claus".

∞ ∞ ∞

Chapter Seven

What a Pantomime!

Christmas time in Primary Schools is a stressful affair for all adults involved. The children are pumped with excitement which makes learning hard for them and teaching harder for the staff. Judith, Dylis and Julie had survived many Christmases since they started work at Lowerdale Primary School. The whole term was the hardest one of the school year because they had so much to pack into a few weeks – including their best attempt at a West End Theatrical extravaganza with a cast which consisted of everyone in the building under the age of thirteen.

All of them had to be happy with the part they were given (never happened), had to learn their lines (rarely happened), sing loudly so that "everyone can hear at the back" (always happened) and bring in a costume from home (varying degrees of success on this score).

The teachers also had to arrange crafts to be made for a Christmas Fair which they had to organize and, at Lowerdale in its role as the centre of the community in a small rural village, they had to invite anyone from the village to come in to school to join the children for a Christmas meal which staff served to everyone. This was a logistical nightmare for all concerned and was a potential child protection nightmare but most of the people who attended were related to the children so everything usually worked out ok. For the Christmas meal, all of the children had to learn carols to perform to the adults and work on poems to be read out before the food was served.

The school had to be decorated for Christmas with only A1 card and whatever glitter was left in the cupboard at the end of the year – plus whatever staff managed to pilfer from home. The Christmas decorations were, by far, the most hated part of the season for the teachers because they had to put it all up all over school then take it all down again at the end of term to go home and do it all over again at home. Plus the sound of Away in a Manger or the shriek of a recorder struggling through Silent Night sends a shiver down every teacher's spine!

The whole over-excited build up and the attempts to maintain some degree of normality in the teaching of the main core subjects is an ultimately exhausting process which leaves the entire staff shell-shocked by the time they peel away the last bit of Blue-tac from the walls where the decorations and children's work had been hung.

Judith, Dylis and Julie felt that, over the years teaching together, they had seen it all. It has been said that nothing can shock a teacher or a solicitor – I know it's certainly true of teachers. However this year was to prove them wrong when June – the new

Head arrived (she was an old Head where she had come from). June had taken on the role from the well-loved and respected retiring Head and had begun at the start of the new academic year in September.

She had seemed nice enough and, despite heavy demands on staff for a massive amount of paperwork (especially in relation to the schools commitment to the environment policy) she had eased into the school without much turbulence. The staff were, therefore, surprised when she dramatically entered the morning assembly one morning dressed as Cruella D'ville (she was fond of unusual outfits which sometimes consisted of very short skirts which wasn't pleasant for the reception children who sat in the middle of the front row) but that particular wardrobe choice was even more flamboyant.

This particular black and white fluffy affair was very eye-catching and the children and adults all locked eyes on her and followed her theatrical flounce across the hall to her chair at the front to address them all. She announced to the children, in a way which visibly struck fear into every one of them, that the entire school was to put on a Christmas play like no other and they MUST follow instruction, DO as they were told, BE the character they were told to be and BRING in what they had to wear ON time AND with everything named.

Judith, Dylis and Julie exchanged discreet eyebrow raises as each of them had children of their own and knew, as parents, how awful it was to have a letter from school informing them that their child would be a donkey in the school play and that they had 3 days to make or buy a costume the like of which would be used in a BBC drama.

June had finished her punctuated list of expectations then addressed the teaching staff to say, on that morning in November, that preparation was to begin that day with ALL of the children remaining in the hall to do carol practice until lunchtime then STAFF MUST MEET AT LUNCHTIME for the hand out and run through of the scripts and then added – this MUST be better than last year's performance and I'm trusting YOU to deliver! Then she left the hall and went back to her office.

For a couple of minutes everyone, staff and children, just sat looking at each other in silence trying to make sense of what had just happened then, as usual, Jared was the first to put his hand in the air to make an enquiry. Despite discretely trying to ignore him, whilst trying to search Christmas carols with lyrics on the internet in a huddle at the computer next to the big screen, Jared was insistent that his inquisitive nature be met with answers and so he stretched higher and waved his arm in the air whilst shouting

Miiiisssss! In the way that every child at home says Muuuum!

Luckily on this occasion poor Jared had only needed to go to the toilet. Unluckily this started the chain reaction which always followed when one child wanted to go to the toilet – a Mexican wave of hands of contenders to go when he'd come back!

Judith organized toilet trips with the military precision that working in schools requires whilst Dylis tried to remove the video she had found for Silent Night with lyrics from the big screen when the video began an advert for Tampax before launching into the carol. Julie, stoically, threw herself in front of the big screen and assumed a star fish stance to attempt to protect the innocent eyes before her from the advert.

However, as the pictures were beamed onto the screen from an overhead projector set up, this merely showed the outline of a tampon hovering dangerously close to her left nostril.

Jared had returned from his ablutions and was waving again to ascertain what the rocket thing was for but Dylis and Julie ignored him completely while Judith ushered the last child back in from the direction of the miniature toilets which, in their miniature cubicles all in a row, were reminiscent of Snow White and the Seven Dwarves.

Having completed operation toilet trot Julie did what all teachers do in times of crisis, much like you would make a cup of hot sweet tea at home, she ran to her classroom to fetch stationery for the three of them. You instantly feel more in control when you're holding a clipboard, a pen and a highlighter in these situations. She passed one each to Judith and Dylis then turned to face the children with her jaw set and her face contorted into a well-used "I mean business" face as if she was at Custer's Last Stand.

She didn't need to say anything (teachers are very good at their own unique version of sign language) she simply raised her palm towards the unruly mob and a calming hush descended. From that point they had managed to get through two attempts at Silent Night and had tried to instill the difference between singing and shouting before the lunchtime supervisors (used to be known as dinner ladies in the dark times of inequality) came in to set up the tables in the hall ready for lunch.

Once the children had washed their hands, decided they needed the toilet, washed their hands again and filed into the hall to take up their position at their assigned tables and seats (carefully selected to reduce risk of an affray) the staff reluctantly assembled in the staff room where June was waiting with a copy of the script for each of them.

The three of them had worked together for so long that they had all grown to share the same thoughts and all three of them looked at the scripts bound in a lever ach file and simultaneously made a "Bless her!" face as they predicted that it didn't matter how well the scripts were presented they would all be lost somewhere along the line before the event and all three of them would end up sharing the one copy in the hope that they would eventually get enough time to stand at the photocopier to fire out two more replicas.

June slid each file to them across the staffroom table like a bar tender would slide a sarsaparilla down the bar in a Western then informed them all that this year would be different (it already was) because she wanted to get rid of the "outdated nativity show" claiming that it had been "done to death" and, instead, wanted to enact the play entitled Humphrey The Camel Has Three Humps. Judith couldn't help herself and snorted with laughter after, wrongly, thinking this a joke but the others could see that June was also a master of the "I mean business" face – it was no joke!

They had listened in silence as June had gone through everything with, what they now knew to be, her trademark punctuation of the important words. When they had been released back into the wild the three of them agreed that they pitied the parents of the poor kid that was given the part of the three-humped camel. They parted ways to their classrooms to have a moment of silence before the bell rang for the children to come back in. Then, like it or not, they all had to knuckle down to the start of what lay ahead and begin the arduous task of casting.

Poor Katrina had been given the starring role of Humphrey for her mother's talents with a needle and thread rather than her own starring qualities then the rest of the children were assigned roles to which each groaned and rolled their eyes. Ultimately nobody was happy. This would prove to be an endurance test for them all!

Progress was made over the next couple of weeks and Judith, Dylis and Julie had managed to pull off some semblance of a play whilst the teaching assistants slaved away on the props and scenery armed with a big white bedding sheet, poster paints and a selection of "junk model-making equipment" or cornflake packets and toilet rolls to those without a teaching degree.

They had all begun to hope that they may be able to pull this off until June came out of her office and into assembly (the staff now knew this to be a bad omen). On this occasion she was wearing a circular cardigan which fell in pretty frills at the side but which wasn't practical school wear because as the breeze, she created from her purposeful stride, caused the sides to lift she got caught up on each table corner as she walked across to the front.

Once there, she announced that this year things would be different (again everyone already realised this) because they would not be performing the school play in school after all – an audible intake of breath and an expectant pause swept the room then was let out with a groan when June announced that she had procured the village hall for not one but two performances instead – a daytime matinee and an evening performance "for those of you with mums and dads that work".

The likelihood of the four year olds of the school surviving this were slim. June had been thrilled to add that the village hall had an actual stage (or potential cliff edge from a child's perspective) then clutched at the edges of her cardigan, to avoid a repeat on the table edges, and swirled it about her like a Machiavellian villain's cape and left the room in stunned silence again.

The remaining days on the lead up to the extravaganza had been chaotic and had left no time for any "normal" lessons. June had expected Cath, a teaching assistant who was nearing retirement to use a fifteen-foot ladder to position a banner in the village hall to say "Welcome to Our Best Ever Production!" But Cath, as she was leaving at Easter, was in a better position than everyone else as she was able to flatly refuse whilst clutching the Health and Safety file which June had updated, reissued and made everyone sign to say they had read it.

June recognized her nemesis and conceded – there would be no banner. Pete, however, the only male member of staff, and one with many years of service remaining rendering him helpless, was given the task of setting up and operating the sound equipment and lighting because he was a man. He had, bravely, attempted Cath's ploy and countered that because he was a man didn't mean that he instinctively knew how to rig up light and sound and murmured "sex discrimination" but retreated from June's "business" face to try to find the microphone.

Rehearsals were frequent and ferocious and the freezing cold walk to and from the hall didn't put the little actors in the best mood for performing. June got involved at this stage and, not only got involved but took charge. She stood in front of the children leaning on a large stick which she'd suddenly revealed and gave the children a speech straight from 'Fame' about being hungry for success and it hurting a lot. Obviously the children were terrified into submission and got on well with the rehearsals.

For the real thing, however, as June had predicted – things were different! Everyone had brought in, tried on and catalogued their costumes ready for the performance and the getting dressed part went without a hitch. They all hurried in from the side of the stage and assumed their positions whilst June did her meet and greet at the doorway until all the adults sat down, then following her brief speech about how the children couldn't wait to show them all what they had done (all lies) she sat on her chair in the middle of the aisle facing the stage and began her role as prompt which actually meant that she just read out everybody's part along with them.

Dylis was assigned the task of children's entertainer in the side room with the reception children until it was their turn to walk on carrying a star then walk off again. Judith was on the left hand side of the stage acting as bouncer for the volatile year Six boys whilst Julie was lay on her side on the floor. She was half under the stage, out of sight, handing the children props discretely. None of them noticed Michael sat at the front of the stage picking his nose all the way through act one till it was his turn or Chloe rush on in a panic thinking she'd missed her line then, more concerning, realizing her shoelace was undone she bent down to tie it while June read her line for her.

There was a part which was meant to be poignant and meaningful at the end which involved a line-up of five of the best readers from Year Six who had to read from a card into a microphone in turn. This went smoothly with the first two children then Lewis dropped the mic on the floor where it landed with a boom followed by feedback then the utterance of a profanity into the mic as James picked it up to the shocked murmurs (and some giggles) from the audience.

The dramatic culmination of the play was marred, further, by Pete using the wrong CD in his hasty attempt to distract the audience from what had just happened and the children bowed and walked off stage to the tune of Star Wars. At that same moment Julie tried to get out from under the stage but had been lying in such an awkward position for the duration of the performance that she couldn't move and, after the first aid trained members of staff decided there could be spinal implications if she was pulled from beneath the stage it was decided that she had to be left there while an ambulance was called to move her safely and check her lumbar region.

June maintained her composure throughout as she ushered the children to their parents and accepted the parents' praise about the show before leaving. Everyone agreed that they'd seen nothing like it before!

∞ ∞ ∞

Chapter Eight

Christmas Beginnings.

I know I had it with me this morning. I must have done because the nice lady on BBC Breakfast News and Weather where I am said I'd need my brolly today. She was right and I'm sure I had it when I left to catch the 89 bus back home again. The monthly catch up with old work mates had been the highlight of my days since I threw away the alarm clock and strapped on my gold watch (for services rendered to the gardening community at the Buttercup Garden Centre in Myton).

People had been so kind and even some of the regular customers had come to share a surprise afternoon tea in my honour on my last day. It had been a day of mixed emotions for me and I had gone home with armfuls of gifts from so many kind folk and sat wondering what to do now as my new found freedom just brought fear of the unknown. For the first time since my wife had passed away – I shed a tear or two.

My favourite "leaving present" had been a rather special thing of wonder from an equally special and wondrous lady – Alice from the Buttercup Tearoom. Round and smiley with twinkly eyes and pink cheeks that always made me feel twinkly too. I loved it when she made a huge fuss of me at tea break each working day. She was what I missed most about not being part of the working masses anymore.

Alice was my sunshine – she always managed to lift my mood without even trying. Nobody else had managed this in the many years since the death of my dear wife. Alice's retirement gift for me had been aptly bright and cheerful – a long umbrella, sunflower in design, with a pointy tip and a wooden curved handle. Big enough for two when its petals opened out and I secretly hoped that one day Alice may shelter with me on a cheery walk on a dreary day by the side of the canal.

Everyone had been envious of the opening of my "new chapter" – my new-found freedom from the daily grind but, since becoming a widow, my workmates and the customers eager to hear my thoughts about the best plant for a dry corner and a heavy soil, were my only company. I enjoyed going to work, despite the aches and pains that slowed my initial start to the day each morning.

By far the best part had been seeing Alice's smiling face as she held out my "usual" sugary brew each morning break. We began to share our lunch breaks which led from debate about sandwich fillings to our shared experiences of grief, loss and loneliness. Her Geoff had died just 2 years after my wife. We both understood each other.

Alice made me feel alive again – I hadn't felt that way since meeting my dear wife as a lad. I felt like I was 18 all over again! Our years working together had flown by so quickly that I hadn't felt the need to question my growing feelings or admit to myself that I would like it if Alice and I could be more than colleagues or even friends. Truth be known, though, I was scared of declaring my feelings in case it spoiled the friendship we had.

So I slipped away from work on my last day with only the knowledge that I would see her, along with all the other staff, in a month's time as we'd all promised to meet monthly to swap news. I had turned up, rain or shine, each month for the past 3 months as had Alice but I still hadn't mustered the courage to ask her if I might be able to see her more frequently and maybe be her companion.

Today's meet up had been no different, though I had rehearsed what I would say to her over and over in my mind before setting off for the Christmas lunch party. When she was there, in front of me, all of my words left me I had made a further bumbling, failed attempt to express my admiration of Alice without making any actual declarations. Angry with myself and embarrassed about my mumblings and bumblings, I had made my excuses about having to rush for the 89 home and left in such a hurry that I had dashed out and somehow lost Alice's leaving present along the way.

It was so upsetting to lose it and I didn't want to retrace my steps in case anybody saw me and found out my hasty departure to be just an excuse to leave rather than a need to dash for a bus. I had to satisfy myself that I would just have to ring the café when I got back home to ask if my brolly had been left there and handed in.

Sat in the bus shelter I regretted my loss – my use to society, my wife, and what might have been with Alice. At this ripe old age how could I be as tongue-tied as I had been in my youth? My future was not bright – another microwaved turkey dinner alone in front of the television on Christmas day. Only darkness and regret to wake to each coming day and I couldn't even get out into my garden because everything was dead and decaying as it did at that time of year.

I pulled my anorak tight round me as I noticed that the weather, as the nice lady on BBC Breakfast had warned, reflected my mood as the chill wind rattled the flimsy bus shelter and the grey skies wept as if in sympathy. Then - she appeared, in a glow of yellow before me, beneath my sunflower saying – 'You left without your brolly! Come on, we can both fit under here if we squeeze in! Looks like you must've missed the bus so why don't we walk back to my house where you can get warm and dry while you wait for the next one?"

I couldn't believe my luck! Here she was before me, alone. This was my chance! But as I tried to force my mouth to sync with my brain she continued 'I've been meaning to ask – I wondered if you might be free on Christmas ? I hate cooking just for one! I'm thinking of retiring early and I'd like your advice too, if you don't mind. I've been unsure about doing it because I'm worried I'll be lonely.'

The End.

Merry Christmas to all and to all a good night!

∞ ∞ ∞

Also by this author:

For The Best?

Do you ever wonder where life could have taken you? How each decision could have taken you down a different path? Most of us will never know, but Sophie knows exactly how her life could have been, and this knowledge haunts her, and tears her family apart until a tragedy forces her to face her demons.

Available to buy through Amazon or direct from the author at www.kdray.co.uk

Printed in Poland
by Amazon Fulfillment
Poland Sp. z o.o., Wrocław